ISBN 0-85079-130-8

Printed in Great Britain

£2.00

RUPERT

"A bonfire! Bingo's started one,"
Cries Rupert. "Ooh, I think they're fun!"

"Hello, Bingo's started a bonfire," thinks Rupert as he crosses Nutwood Common one morning. "Oh, good!" And he hurries across to find his pal Bingo, the clever pup, stirring up a large bonfire. "Oo, can I help?" Rupert pleads. "We won't be burning leaves this year. We're keeping them to do the garden good later." Bingo smiles. "Help if you like," he says. "But I think I know something you'll like better than messing

This Book Belongs To:

CONTENTS

Why not cut out a snapshot of yourself to fit the circle above?

and the Black Circle

"There is a mystery," says the pup,
"That someone like you might clear up."

"Some strangers' talk I overheard,
But didn't understand a word."

about with a bonfire." Rupert waits. "You're fond of mysteries, aren't you?" says Bingo. "Well, as I was coming through the woods just now I heard weird voices but I couldn't see anyone. They weren't speaking English or Gipsy or anything I've heard before." Of course, Bingo is right. Rupert can't resist mysteries and as soon as his chum has pointed the direction the little bear hurries away towards the trees.

So Rupert hurries off to seek
The folk who this strange language speak.

RUPERT SEES THE STRANGERS

His search takes Rupert up a hill
Where someone calls, "Hi, look!" It's Bill.

"Mysterious strangers down below,"
Says Bill. "Look, Rupert, there they go!"

"Let's see if they're the foreign band
That Bingo couldn't understand."

Then Reggie Rabbit hails our pair.
He looks as if he's had a scare.

Rupert works his way through a corner of the wood without seeing or hearing anything strange. Then a call makes him turn. His pal, Bill Badger, is beckoning to him. "What's up?" asks Rupert as he joins him at the fence. "Such strange people have been passing along the track down there," says Bill. "Look, there's another lot." Sure enough, a wagon and caravan and some men with their horses are slowly entering a distant part of the forest. Now seems the time for Rupert to tell Bill of Bingo and the voices. "Well, that lot are certainly strangers. They may be the ones Bingo heard," says Bill. "Come on then, let's get a bit nearer to them." They cross the fence and scamper downhill to enter the wood beside the track. Almost at once there is the sound of someone running fast and next moment Reggie Rabbit appears through the trees. He scurries straight for them. "Whatever's the matter?" asks Rupert. "You look quite scared."

RUPERT STARTS TO SEARCH

Wails timid Reggie in dismay,
"Weird foreigners are on their way."

Then as the strange dark men they see,
The three chums hide behind a tree.

"Come on," cries Rupert, "let's find out
Just what those strangers are about!"

But Reggie is too scared and so
He stays while on the others go.

"I am a bit scared," admits Reggie. "There's a crowd of foreigners coming this way. I don't like the look of them." "What *more* of them?" cries Rupert. "Not so loud," quavers Reggie. And the three of them dodge into some bushes just in time to avoid being seen by the procession that files past talking in a strange language. "Look at their clothes," hisses Bill. "Who can they be?" Rupert breathes. Reggie says nothing, but Rupert and Bill are now excited. "We must find out more about them," Bill says. "Let's keep under cover and stalk them." "What an awful idea," Reggie whimpers. "Think what they might do if they caught us! I've had enough." And away he runs. "Never mind him," Rupert grins. "Let's work round this little hill. We should be able to reach another point of the track before the strangers get there." Bill likes the idea and so the two pals move off quickly, taking care not to be seen.

Rupert and the Black Circle

RUPERT IS TEASED

"I thought that band would come by here,"
Says Bill. "But I was wrong, I fear."

"Have you seen strange folk?" Rupert begs.
The man just grins and pulls their legs.

"Seriously, though, I've seen no tribe,"
The man says, "such as you describe."

"There's Gaffer Jarge. Perhaps he's seen
That band when on his rounds he's been."

As Rupert expected, he and Bill reach the track again much further on and for a while they wait in hiding for the mysterious strangers to appear. They wait and wait but no one comes and at last they give up. "They must have turned off somewhere," says Rupert. "Let's ask that man if he's seen them." The man listens to them with a twinkle in his eye. "Weird? Strange clothes?" he repeats. "Oh, ay, they're behind every hedge around here. We keep them for scaring birds!" Rupert and Bill gape. Then Bill notices the grin on the man's face. "Oh, come on, you're teasing," he cries. "Please tell us if you've seen any foreign people passing here." "Nay," says the man. "Either you're pulling my leg or else something odd is happening. There've been no strangers past my farm." Thanking him, the pals move on. "This really is a mystery," declares Rupert. "Look, there's Gaffer Jarge by that gate. He may have seen them."

RUPERT ASKS GAFFER JARGE

*"We wondered if you'd chanced to spy
Some folk like Indians go by?"*

*Their question makes the Gaffer scoff,
"I've got no time for games. Be off!"*

*"So far our search has been no good.
That band must still be in the wood."*

*At home that evening Mr. Bear
Says, "Yes, search on. But do take care."*

Rupert climbs on to the gate beside the old man. "Please, have you seen some people rather like Indians go past?" he asks. "What's that?" wheezes Gaffer Jarge. "I be too old to play Red Injuns, young Rupert." "No, not Red Indians—real ones," Bill explains. "And this isn't a game." "Oh, gwan with 'ee!" growls the old man. "Don't believe there be any such round here. Be off with 'ee and play your tricks elsewhere." The pals look at each other. "Well, we haven't found out much," says Rupert. "Those strangers have either turned off to another village or they are still in the forest. But why? And who are they?" But now both are getting hungry so after arranging to meet Bill next day, Rupert hurries home and tells his Daddy all that has happened. "And I may go with Bill again, mayn't I?" he asks. Mr. Bear is not too keen on the idea but after Rupert has promised to be careful he agrees. "But don't be too inquisitive," he warns.

RUPERT FINDS A BLACK CIRCLE

"I hope," says Willie Mouse, "that you
Can think of something we might do."

"Mysterious strangers lurk down there.
Help find them," asks the little bear.

At the Anteater residence
He spies a strange mark on the fence.

Then Mr. Anteater appears.
Sees Rupert. Stops. And crossly peers.

Soon after starting next day Rupert meets his friend Willie Mouse. "Hello," says Willie. "I hoped I'd meet you. I can't think of anything to do." "Why not join us in solving a mystery?" says Rupert eagerly, and leading Willie to a ridge he points to the woods and tells him all about the mysterious strangers. "You go in there and see if you can discover anything," he says, "and I'll fetch Bill." "Y-yes, all right," Willie agrees nervously. Then, as he agreed the day before, Rupert hurries off to meet Bill. On his way a mark on a fence catches his eye. It is round and nearly black. "Now, who's been doing that?" he wonders. "I do believe that's the back fence of old Mr. Anteater's garden. He *will* be angry when he sees that." And a little further on who should he see but Mr. Anteater himself striding along looking very annoyed indeed. Out of the corner of his eye he catches sight of Rupert. He stops and turns abruptly to face the little bear.

RUPERT TELLS MR. ANTEATER

"Marks on my gate!" he storms. "Now you
Tell me they're on my back fence too!"

As they return the mark to view,
They see that Bill has found it too.

Outside Mr. Anteater's house
Who should run up but Willie Mouse.

"Why," Willie says, "I've seen that mark
There, on a tree, burned in the bark."

Mr. Anteater looks furious. "I was going to find Constable Growler," he storms, "but maybe you can tell me what I want to know. Someone has put a dirty black ring on my front gate. Have you young rascals been up to mischief?" Rupert stares. "On your front gate?" he repeats. "I've just seen a black circle on your back fence, too. But we didn't make them. May I see the other one?" They turn back and find Bill gazing at the new mark. Bill has no idea either how the black circles appeared. Then just as Mr. Anteater is turning to go to Constable Growler there is a patter of feet and Willie Mouse runs up to join them. "I didn't like being alone in the woods in case those mysterious strangers found me," he says, "so I came out. But what are you all looking so solemn about?" They show him the mark and he gives a start. "That's weird!" he exclaims. "I've just seen a ring like that a very short time ago. It was on a tree in the woods."

Rupert and the Black Circle

RUPERT IS SHOWN MORE MARKS

The pals dash off to see the tree
And hope they'll solve the mystery.

"You see! It's the same sort of thing.
A black and sooty kind of ring."

Up scampers Reggie Rabbit and
Asks if they've found the foreign band.

"Black rings?" cries Reggie. "Just in there
On trees I found another pair!"

"So those marks are not only on my property," says Mr. Anteater. "What can it mean?" "This looks like *another* mystery!" cries Rupert. "May we try to find out where the black rings are coming from?" "Very well," Mr. Anteater agrees. "If you can solve it I need not worry Constable Growler." So, led by Willie, the pals hurry into the woods and there, just as he said, they find a rough dark circle on the smooth bark of a tree. Rupert is very puzzled. "Those marks are all different sizes, but they are all rings," he muses. "What can they be?" As he speaks the figure of Reggie Rabbit appears again. "I just had to come back and see if there was any more sign of those strangers who passed yesterday," he says. "We haven't heard or seen them," Rupert tells him. "But now there's another mystery—black circles appearing all over the place." Reggie stares. "Black circles?" he breathes. "Oh dear, I've just seen two black circles. Both on trees!"

Rupert and the Black Circle

RUPERT FORMS A SECRET BAND

Agog, the searchers gather round
The rings that Reggie Rabbit's found.

"That's it!" cries Rupert. "Now I see!
It's some secret society!"

Now Reggie's really had a scare.
To join the hunt he doesn't care.

So off to find a place they troop
Where they can form their secret group.

Soon the others are examining the rings Reggie has found. "They are sinister, aren't they?" he quavers. "I don't think I shall stay here. I don't like all this. First those strangers and now black circles." What he says makes Rupert start. "That's it. The Black Circle!" he cries. "Those foreigners are probably a secret society—spies perhaps—and they're called the Black Circle and those rings are their secret sign! That would explain everything!" And that does it for Reggie. With a squeak of dismay he scuttles away out of the woods. Rupert, though, is quite carried away by his own idea. "What we should do," he says, "is form another secret society and spy on *them*." This is just the sort of idea that appeals to Bill. "That's a splendid idea!" he cries. "First we must find some secret spot for our meeting place." So he and Rupert push deeper into the woods in search of such a place. Willie follows. But rather nervously.

Rupert and the Black Circle

RUPERT'S PAL MAKES A FIND

*"This can be our society's den.
From here we'll look out for those men."*

*Bill and Rupert turn to stare
As Willie cries, "What's that down there?"*

*He runs across and from the ground
Picks something up. What has he found?*

*They closely study Willie's find.
A ball—but not the usual kind.*

Deep in the woods the friends come to a stop. "This will do for a den," says Rupert. "It's close to the track and by looking through the branches we'll be able to see other people though they can't see us." "But we still don't know where those strangers are," Bill says. "We'd better scout round." So they creep out to look and listen. Suddenly Willie Mouse stiffens and peers ahead. "What's the matter?" whispers Rupert. "Has he heard something?" Willie catches Rupert's whisper. "No," he says. "But I've seen something." And he darts forward to pick an object out of the grass. "I say, that's a jolly good ball," says Rupert. "But what curious marks on it." "It was on the track where the mysterious strangers were," exclaims Bill as an idea suddenly strikes him. "Perhaps those are the magic signs of the secret society. Though, I must admit, the circles aren't black." "Let's think about this," Rupert murmurs. "It may well be an important clue."

RUPERT GIVES THE GAME AWAY

"No, not an ordinary ball.
Look! Hardly any bounce at all."

Then suddenly Bill cries, "I say,
There's someone coming down this way."

Into their den the three chums leap,
And, fearful, through the branches peep.

It's just as well the one who comes
Is Bingo, for he spies the chums.

Rupert studies Willie's find closely. "It doesn't make my fingers tingle," he says. "So I don't think it can be a magic ball. But I'm sure it isn't an ordinary one. It's too heavy and, look, it doesn't bounce well. Perhaps we can have a game with it when we've solved the mystery of the Black Circle." As he speaks, Bill turns sharply. "Hush! Someone's coming!" he says. Willie seizes the ball and the three scurry into their den. And there they crouch, excited and wondering who will appear. "Oh, bother!" whispers Rupert. "I believe I'm going to sneeze." Frantically he tries to stop it. But no luck. "It's no good. I can't stop it!" he chokes. "A-a-choo!" Unknown to the others the person they are hiding from is none other than their friend Bingo, the brainy pup. The loud sneeze behind the tree so close to him really makes him jump. "What on earth was that?" he cries and swings round.

RUPERT TELLS BINGO

"I never would have found your den
If Rupert hadn't sneezed just then."

"That tongue you couldn't understand
Belongs to the Black Circle band!"

"See this black ring here on the tree,
The sign of their society!"

But Bingo when he sees the mark
Sits down and guffaws: "What a lark!"

After Rupert's sneeze the three cower and hold their breath. In vain. Their hiding place is discovered and somebody peers in. "Why, it's only Bingo!" cries Willie. Bingo stares. "What on earth are you three doing there?" he demands. Laughing with relief they scramble out and face him. "Why don't you join us?" Rupert asks. "We're trying to track down those strangers you heard yesterday. We actually saw them but now they've disappeared." Bingo gets excited when he hears this. "But why do you have to have a secret society to stalk them?" he wants to know. "Because," Rupert says earnestly, "we believe they're a gang of foreign spies known as the Black Circle and that they've been putting their secret sign, a black ring, on trees and fences all over the place." "Yes, here's one!" says Bill, pointing to a tree. Bingo looks at the mark. Then to their amazement he sits down and laughs and laughs.